The Blessing of Children

And Other Stories

Simon Yarty

Copyright 2019 by Simon Yarty

All rights reserved. This book or any portion thereof may not be reproduced or used in any manner whatsoever without the express written permission of the publisher except for the use of brief quotations in a book review.

Contents

Kastle..1

Jobsworth...9

Inflation..29

Biscuit Tin..37

The Blessing of Children...53

Assisted Living...63

Deadlock..77

Kastle

Mary Kay had lived alone for twenty-two years in various locations in Devon since her husband had died at the age of thirty-seven. She currently lived in a rented one-bedroom maisonette in the near coastal East Devon village of Branscombe and in order to get by, worked two jobs for a total of thirty hours per week at minimum wage. Her home was an annexe to her landlord's house, two large rooms on the ground floor and two above and she had lived in the village for three years, moving from her last place in Exeter when she had got a full-time packing job in Shafers on the Heathpark Industrial Estate at Honiton. That job had come to an end six months ago when she had failed to return from annual leave due, she said in a telephone call to her manager, to the Polish women not speaking to her and her being unable to work in an environment as unfriendly as that. The reason for the move was to find a place she could eventually retire to. Branscombe was her choice. It couldn't be Bude. And the job at Honiton gave her just enough above rent, utility bills and food to afford to run a car. Since leaving Shafers she had sold her car. In the months following she had managed to pick up four six hour shifts at Frydays in Seaton and five hours weekend cleaning at the Mason's

Arms in the village. With March coming to a close she was hoping to pick up more hours as the tourist season accelerated.

It was Saturday afternoon and having finished her shift in the pub the remainder of the day belonged to her. Billy, her elderly cairn terrier, lay sleeping in her armchair. She had got him from a shelter in Exeter just after she had moved and had initially left him with a dog minder when she was at work but for some time now she had kept him at the house and had set up a large litter tray for him near the back door. She sighed, picked up her mug and an unopened letter she didn't want to think about and carried them through to the kitchen where she added it to a small pile of similar looking letters. Outside, the patio flags of her courtyard garden were dry and the milk-white sky seemed benign and breathless as though weather had fixed still for the day. She was humming along to Dolly Parton singing It's all Wrong But it's All Right and just for a moment she thought about Norman Cowell the bus driver who lived on Locksey's Lane with his wife and two adult sons who sometimes flirted with her when she travelled to Seaton. She rinsed her mug and placed it on the drainer. It was time to take a walk, but she was reluctant and kept finding other small tasks to do.

Downstairs the house was arranged to have a front door opening into the reception room. She had her table and two chairs up against the window with a small television stand to the side in the corner, with a CD player beneath. Looking into the room from the front window there were two armchairs against the party wall, opposite the fireplace with a small side cabinet beyond that. The L-shaped stair case marked the division to the kitchen where there had presumably been an interior wall previously. On her cabinet was a tray of wine glasses and a small group of framed photographs, the walls were bare, finding things to hang was still on her mental list of projects to complete. In the kitchen she had a cork notice board where she pinned her lists and leaflets of village and other events, including an invitation to the wedding of a friend in April which she would not be going to. Upstairs, where Mary now went, there was a large blue and white tiled floor bathroom with separate shower and a double bedroom at the front of the house. In the bathroom she checked herself in the mirror. Sixty-two now but she felt she could pass for being in her fifties, her shoulder-length hair was blonde with copper tones, a colour that suited her light complexion and dark blue eyes. She was a little larger now than she had ever been but weight had always been a struggle at her small height of only five foot six inches and much of it had always settled on her thighs and bottom leaving her thin at the waist and slender in the shoulders and arms. She had never been comfortable with her shape. Her face and neck were a little fleshy but her lips were full and one of her best features, she thought. She noticed she was frowning and smiled at herself but was dismayed at how many wrinkles this activated around her eyes and mouth. She put on her makeup.

Mary believed that she had only been in love once and she had married him. Jamie Kay, at the age of twenty-two in the registry office at Tavistock on a Wednesday morning at the beginning of a deathly hot June. At that time he was working as a delivery driver and she was working nights at a factory a few miles outside the town, but one day they would run their own cafe together and work side by side. They never did of course, that is just the nature of shared dreams, you build something to share, she knew that. Jamie had a temper and would often have arguments at work and end up looking for another job every six months or so. She coped with this because he was essentially a good man, they rarely argued themselves but he always wanted more for them than they had and wanted it quickly. In the eighteen years or so they were together they must have moved home a dozen times, lived in a variety of towns and villages and had different jobs every year.

He would sometimes drink too much and throw away what little money they had on schemes and ventures, like a van to start his own delivery business or stock for him to sell at Exeter Market, but these things had always failed and she always forgave him, they were young, he was young and she would have a lifetime to fix him. He belonged to her and she knew he loved her more than his own life and because of that nothing else mattered.

In the bedroom Mary changed into a pair of blue jeans, her white woollen sweater, a pair of trainers and took her black quilted raincoat from the wardrobe. She picked up her handbag off the dresser where it had sat next to a small etched glass bowl with two rings in it. She checked the bag's contents and went downstairs to fetch the dog leash from the kitchen. "Billy boy!" She called and the dog appeared limping eagerly toward her. "Would you like to take a walk?" She asked and Billy yapped. She opened the door onto Mill Lane and turned left towards the footpath that would eventually lead her to the coast.

Her life had not stopped with the death of her husband, she had taken up a number of relationships in the years that had passed since the horror of that evening twenty-two years ago. Often these had involved married men, alcohol and off-peak sex. But now and again there was a man worth spending her time with. Things would often start well, a walk, a picnic, a drive to Exmouth or her beloved Bude, but fail in small things. She needed them to have more going on in their heads than they had. She needed them to make her feel things again. But they only ever talked about themselves. As though they ever could have had interesting lives. And quickly her interest always diminished. Anyway, that had all stopped when she moved to the village, she wasn't expecting it to happen to her any more.

At the public footpath she unclasped the dog lead and told Billy to "go on" but as usual he didn't. His arthritis was so severe now he just walked beside her. Looking up at her now and again wondering if he had done enough to be carried, but she wasn't going to do that today. In a mile or so she knew he would start whimpering as the pain in his legs got too much for him to cope with. They crossed the first green field together. The wind had started to pick up and she stopped to zip up her coat against the waves of cold air. The breeze was making her eyes water and she squinted ahead of her as the next field rose gently up to the white of the sky. They were going to call it Kastle, their cafe, or whatever it was to be. The menus changed when she and Jamie had imagined their own business. She was cream tea and cakes to his cooked breakfasts and sandwiches but she liked the joy in coming up with names, and how it changed with every joke they made about it.

It would be on the front at Bude of course, with yellow-topped tables inside and on the pavement, with cornflower blue painted wooden chairs. They would open the place together six mornings a week under deep blue skies and a sun that would make them sweat at nine in the morning. Each day they would mock each other until their ribs hurt from laughing and they would make love every night until they were too old for the exertion. She would taste sugar and salt on his lips and know she had made real in her life what others only understand is important when it is too late.

At the brow of the hill the path led through a clump of trees before opening again to another field, at the bottom of which ran the South West Coastal Path. Emerging from the trees she looked out at the big grey sea. She sat down on a mound. To her left she could see Seaton and beyond that Lyme and the cream white rock face of West Bay far in the distance. To her right she could just see the tiny rooftops of Sidmouth.

She was crying as she took her hair band from her bag and quickly slipped it over Billy's jaws, she pulled the plastic bag over his head and hugged him tightly to her chest so that he couldn't struggle free. She did not have the money to take him to the vets at Seaton. That she had lived to this age, had always worked, had no expensive vices yet was still always a week's pay away from being broke seemed unfair, even cruel. She inhaled the familiar smell of Billy's fur and could feel his little heart thump against his ribs and all the time his growling and whining made her cry harder.

She would be truly alone and unloved now, she would be apart from everything, friendless and childless. "I'm sorry Billy," she whispered, "I'm sorry my love."

As she fell deeper into herself and into misery and as Billy struggled less she thought about the night Jamie died. They had a ground floor flat on Blundell's Road in Tiverton, she was working swing shifts for a company on the Howden Estate and he had been out of work for a fortnight. She had finished early on that Friday afternoon and bought them cans of lager and fish and chips. They were watching television together and he said his head was really hurting. She told him to get some paracetamol but when he tried to stand up he fell on his knees and then he just seemed to lose balance as he swayed over, his head hitting the floor first. She sat for a second in shock and then the terror rose when she realised he was unconscious and though she stroked his face and said "Jamie, my love" over and over she couldn't wake him. The paramedics took them to Exeter and less than twenty-four hours later she agreed for life support to be switched off. She had gone from everything to nothing in one day. But that second day, the day after his death, the day she could no longer talk to him, see his face, hear him tell his bad jokes, that day had been her worst day.

Billy had stopped struggling and she could no longer feel the pound of his heart, she carried him carefully the few yards back to the tree line and began to look for a suitable place to leave him. She found a good spot about fifty yards from the path, scraped a little area of top soil with a sharp edged stone and lay him down. She took the bag and hair band off him sobbing at the sight of his wild terrified eyes, she undid his collar and stuffed it in her bag. Then she covered him in leaves, soil and twigs. She had said goodbye to Jamie in private before the machine was switched off. She had put her hand on his cheek and said "I don't know what happens next Jamie, I love you so much." But the things that happened next were not extraordinary. With Jamie life had been heightened, filmic. With him she lived entirely in the present as though past or future were just things they made from what they were doing at that very moment. But she never felt that again. "Goodbye Billy, my boy." She said as she left for the path.

It was getting dark as Mary got to the last field before the village. On the way back she had composed a list of things to do. She would find another job or some extra hours. She would make an effort to get into village life more, perhaps volunteer her time, join some clubs. She shivered as she got back to Mill Lane and put her hands into the pockets of her coat and clutched the cold wet steel of the dog chain.

Jobsworth

David Leicester sat in his chair while his computer booted itself up. He was the current University Admissions Officer at Sussex, prior to that the senior clerical officer in the Faculty of Arts at London Met. Thirty-eight now and behind where he should have been in his career. A Grade Three when he should have been a Five — the equivalent of a senior lecturer. He knew that a promotion wouldn't even require a reorganisation, just a sympathetic review of his responsibilities, just as he knew that the Registrar would never invite Human Resources to do it. He sat at his desk looking out at his aspect of the campus, the flat-roofed student shop and the three flights of stairs down to the grey academic buildings, and in the centre of the quadrangle the newly planted yew trees hemmed in like lost children by public benches where the pond used to be. He used to sit by it on summer lunch breaks while he plotted out his career.

At 10am on each Monday of the academic year the senior management team of the Academic Registry met to discuss the previous week's meeting. At various points section heads were summoned, he was normally called first unless Degree Conferments were imminent but always ahead of Student Records, Assessment and Quality. The Registrar, Mr Jonathan Richards, was ex-BBC, he had been told. His interest was in the reputation of his department, operations were delegated to his two senior assistants and he frequently had a reason to exit any meeting before it reached its conclusion. The Registrar's office was large with a view of the main entrance to the campus, two black leather sofas and a large dark wood table with neat stacks of papers and folders carefully arranged. "David, sit, please" he said. "I know Shelagh and Tony have some technical questions on where the Deans have moved to with regard to recruitment targets but I just wanted to begin by recalling that Senate agreed at its last meeting that the University needed to remain especially mindful of entry qualification averages in its cohorts."

"Well," replied David, "the new admission tutor forum I have recently established is currently drafting some proposals for Clearing which I should be able to tweak soon." While everybody grinned at each other he helped himself to coffee. He had spent a lot of time assessing his colleagues. Richards was in his early sixties, always in a black suit and alternating between blue and red ties, of a medium height, short white side-parted hair and gut he couldn't quite hide behind the one button of his jacket. His talent, it seemed to him and everyone, including the Registrar, was public speaking, but in a mannered, rehearsed style. His eyes were energetic, always gauging the faces of senior people within a room, monitoring each cadence in his performance. He often wondered what the University gained in return for its spending on Richards. In contrast, to his left sat Shelagh Darke, Senior Assistant Registrar (Systems) who was tenacious on the details of any administrative task she was asked to oversee but known to be underdeveloped in her people skills. In her fifties, quiet, small framed with short grey hair, a former deputy head teacher in a London secondary school whom Richards seemed to look down upon for two reasons; her lack of wit in oratory and that she was, quite recently, an internal promotion.

To his right, Tony Hastings, Senior Assistant Registrar (Services), a lesser version of Richards, previously an Assistant Registrar at UCL, also in his fifties, good-humoured and by all that he had heard from others competent and supportive. David slipped his way past questions on targets and rose as the Registrar thanked him for giving up his time. As he was about to leave Richards asked how Professor Allen, Dean of Science was preparing for the next year. "Hands on as always. I expect him to be in every meeting I go to."

That last question perhaps inferred that his colleagues knew that he was to have an interview for the School Manager post in Science. He would go and see Shelagh and see if anything fell out. It was not a position he really wanted, it was too much of a detour. Leverage maybe, but only if he figured in Registry's long-term plans. He had applied when Professor Allen had told him that none of his own team were up to it.

He was a long way from the future he imagined for himself when growing up in Cheadle Hulme. He had spent a year after A Levels and before he went to Manchester University for his degree in Business Administration, reading the books he assumed he should know, working on reducing his accent. He thought he would be self-employed. Importing something to sell or at least offering some form of business consultancy. Nearly twenty years later and he realised that he had let too many years slip by without ever really challenging himself. His old life was gone now. No friends or contacts remained from before he went to university. He saw his parents every other Christmas, they were close to retirement. His mother did clerical work at an accountants and his father was a salesman for a plastics company. To his mind he had moved class, a data point above the line of the Great Gatsby Curve. In his frequent bouts of self-evaluation he often concluded that he was the type who made things happen in a workplace. If not yet a leader then at least a facilitator for them. In post for four years, he had encouraged significant revisions to the admissions process each year in order to bring schools and central administration closer. There were now more cross-disciplinary panels and working groups than the university had known for some time. Admissions was coherent at Sussex, there was a decent system and good communication and much of this was a result of his persistence. But still he had to watch as others progressed and he did not. When the less accomplished lofted above him it was difficult to have faith in meritocracy, without it as the accelerant then career progression was reduced to the whims of senior managers. On returning to his office he opened the internal door to his operations room where his three staff worked and asked Lindsay to come through.

"We need to chase up Professor Ellis about increasing social sciences by 50 to 60 ftes, see where they are on their new joint course proposals."

"I don't think they have got very far," Lindsay replied. "I'm meeting Sue from their School Office for lunch so I can find out the gossip."

"Good. Have International fed in their targets yet?"

"Still waiting."

Of his three staff Lindsay was clearly the one who would have a career. Late twenties, twenty-nine he recalled. She was a favourite of Richards, a graduate from Sussex who had lapsed from postgraduate studies to take a position in the Student Records Office, before moving to admissions as his spreadsheet person. Not to say that he thought badly of his other staff; John who liaised on marketing through to enrolment and Hilary who more or less ran the office, but it was Lindsay who he could give the more subtle tasks to, and she simply understood what he was trying to do without needing to have it explained. She was single as far as he knew, tall and shapely, funny, always cheerful and quite cultured, which disconcerted him a little. She could throw references to operas and novels into a conversation where he then had to either bluff or change the topic. She hadn't been to private school but her parents were both professionals, or perhaps it was just her father who was in law, he wasn't sure. Recently though, he had noticed she was less bright, pre-occupied and a little absent. "You look like you need a holiday if you don't mind me saying Lindsay, either that or we need another office night out soon."

"Yes", she replied, "the only problem with that is that none of you know how to drink and by 10 o'clock you've all sloped off. And that's just rude."

He laughed, thought about how much he hated his ninety-minute commute and knew he wouldn't be arranging a night out in the near future.

After lunch at his desk he called to see if Shelagh was free for a catch-up. As a consequence of the high profile of Admissions and unusually for his post grade he reported directly to the Registrar. While he accepted, even at times enjoyed this arrangement, he also respected Shelagh's experience and in return for his deferring to her as an unofficial line manager he had made her into an ally. Though until this moment it had not extended to him discussing his career with her.

Shelagh Darke was not a go-to person in the central administration. She struggled with small talk, and most staff came away from meeting her thinking her aloof, even abrasive. In working groups and committees her colleagues concentrated especially hard in order to avoid being verbally eviscerated in front of their friends. She generated the type of fear you feel when you realise that you are not actually very good at something and briefly wonder why you draw such a big salary. If Shelagh carried on dissecting your work efforts in a group session then soon the whole university would discover that you were an idiot. If you had been briefed before meeting her you would be surprised that she was such a slight woman, prematurely aged in some respects, so wrinkled around the eyes was she, and think that you could just walk or talk straight through her. She appeared friendly on first greeting but then became so reserved that you would never offer your hand. Of the two Senior Assistant Registrars it had been made materially clear she was the junior. Her office was furthest down the corridor from the Registrar's and probably smaller than his own, a little dark rectangle with her desk beneath the window with blinds always down, cabinets of papers the length of both walls and an uncomfortable grey plastic chair in front of her for visitors. Her secretary, Alice, had an even smaller adjacent room which barely had room for a desk as it stored yet more cabinets.

"Sit. With you in a moment." She said while tapping at away at her keyboard. "Ha!" She exclaimed as she worked and gave the keyboard a last big flurry of fingers before smiling broadly at her computer screen.

"There. How are you?"

"Well," David replied, "Apprehensive, but well."

"Why so?" she asked, sitting back into her chair.

"I should perhaps have mentioned the interview I have in Science tomorrow."

Shelagh paused and smiled again. "No need. You've done what? Five years? It is about the right time. You do the hard work and you have some talent. Good luck."

They were both silent for slightly too long. Shelagh's smile became fixed.

"Do you ever feel," David continued, "that something is not quite right with careers here? Those who work hard and are more than able don't seem to get the reward."

"No. Never whinge. You put your wins on your record, you keep your C.V. up to date with your achievements, and if you leave you get someone like me to put an open letter in your HR file. In any case, we make our own futures. You use everything to get where you should be. I don't believe in karma. Too many long-lived wastes of life out there for there to be any truth in that sort of thing."

On the drive from Falmer to St Albans he again thought about where he stood in his career. His

Strength, he thought, was that unlike many of his colleagues he was able to master process and detail whilst also being an excellent communicator. His self-control was sound, he knew how and when to contribute at committee and when to let things pass. He could not easily find **W**eaknesses in himself. In terms of his standing, yes, he was too junior to have significant academic allies with the one exception of Professor Allen. **O**pportunities, well, he had been ready for promotion for at least two years but he did not want to move institutions again and the current Registry senior managers looked set to work to retirement. This was another reason why he had applied for the School Manager job. The lack of turnover among senior Registry staff and having to move out from the centre of the university were his career **T**hreats. He had a feeling though, that even if he were successful tomorrow it wouldn't make him happy, he wanted to be a University Registrar within ten years, messing about with academics who wanted to be managers wasn't going to help him get there.

When he opened the door to his three-bedroom semi-detached home it had gone 7pm, his four year old daughter Lily, still up and lively, ran to him and hugged him. Sarah called him to the kitchen and kissed him on the lips. She was tall, thin and confident, her long black hair tied back neatly. She owned her own letting agency in St Albans which she had called Church Lets. Church being her maiden name. They had met when they were both twenty-three, she had been in business a year making use of an inheritance from her father who had died of cancer the year before. He remembered how intimidated he had felt when she told him what she did for a living. Even now he struggled with how to talk about his time at work, universities being such medieval places, so that in the end he rarely talked about the ups and downs of his day.

"Salad?" He asked sadly.

"You will thank me." She replied, placing a plate on the table before pouring herself a large glass of red wine.

"Wine?" He said hopefully. Sarah shook her head.

"You are not a nice person." He laughed.

He sat down and while reaching for a fork Lily slid a piece of paper over his meal.

"I drew that." She declared, beaming.

David looked at the splodges of colour and incomprehensible tornadoes of heavy pencilling. "It's wonderful, honey, how long did it take?"

"I've got more." Lily answered.

At home his ambitions had a different pattern. Here they covered facts like why they were not yet living in a detached house, out of town, with a large garden. Why didn't they have better cars, take better holidays. Eat out at restaurants, go to plays. Own a holiday cottage anywhere in Cornwall, buy new clothes every week. For all of this that he felt was lacking he blamed himself, but he also kept a fragment of the blame back for Sarah. While it gave her freedom her business rarely delivered much more than he earned and she seemed content with that. She saw no reason to open another branch. Sex had slipped to fortnightly. Neither of them was at fault, it had just happened. If he got his career back to where it should be it would probably fix most of their problems.

They watched television. Sarah put Lily to bed and when they went up for the night they both lay awake. "Are you worried about tomorrow?" Sarah asked, her hand stroking his shoulder.

"Not really," he replied, "I should get it, there is no competition from internal applicants and they won't get an external who knows how the centre works better than me."

"So, what is it then?"

"I don't know. Lately, I've been thinking If I was destined to have a brilliant career then I'd have a brilliant career and not just be some junior middle manager."

"What about looking at other universities?"

"I do look, but it has to have the right set up, the institution needs to have a large centralised admissions service to stand any chance of it being lead by a Grade Five. And then there is the distance from St Albans."

Sarah sighed "You know I would pack it all in and move."

"I know," David replied, kissing her on the cheek. "I don't want you to do that."

He shaved cautiously to avoid any nicks. He looked at his reflection. Fifteen stone last time he had weighed himself. No grey or white hairs among the black yet but still receding. His face looked bloated when it was not in motion. He turned to see what he looked like in profile and pulled a face at himself. His hair was too long for someone with a growing bald patch and his stomach was starting to drop. He patted his face dry. He had already picked out his black suit, a pale blue shirt and dark blue tie, and had laid them out on his side of the bed.

"What time is it baby?" Asked Sarah from beneath the covers.

"Just after 6am, go back to sleep."

"Good luck darling."

On the drive to Falmer he normally listened to Radio 4 in an effort to take himself out of his typical range of thoughts. He needed to be upbeat and personable today and being engrossed in himself wouldn't be a good look. In any case it was always useful to keep up with current affairs as well as educational news, he would not survive long in his post without conversation skills, he could not afford to be without opinions.

"David." The Dean welcomed him.

"Andrew" He replied warmly and took the offered seat. He realised that he was not nervous. He looked around at the panel he was about to be introduced to. He knew them all and could not imagine working for any of them. With the exception of the Dean he could not see any satisfaction in working for an academic. It was not their fault that their view of administrators came over as one of contempt. It wasn't really that. To them administration was a resource they bid for and when won it was co-opted to whatever project they were working on and it did what it was told. It existed to both support them locally and to be demonised in the centre of the university. Administrators were just a top-slice off income, all of which was generated by academics. In this location, David thought, there was no such thing as university, just the subject, and a cluster of academic egos. Professor Allen sat at the head of the school conference table. He was enjoying this. A tall thin man in his forties, near bald. A Chemist by discipline and highly cited in his research. This and his ability to communicate with anyone, even administrators had enabled his rise in academic management. It seemed effortless from the outside, as though he had to be dragged into taking up management roles, persuaded to chair a committee or two, encouraged to lead a working group. Yet David knew none of that was true, this was a relatively young and amiable but above all ambitious Dean.

After insisting David go through the routine of matching his C.V. to the essential experience requirements of the job specification he let his colleagues go for a meander beyond the job description but once it was obvious to Professor Allen that his candidate was starting to become exasperated by the idiocy of some of the questions, he pulled them back. All the time the smile that betrayed his enjoyment was unhidden on his face. On and on it went. He was beginning to wonder if he was the only interviewee.

"Finally David, before we let you ask us a few questions, I have a last one. What do you think the purpose of academic management is and how can a good administrator best assist in that?"

"Well, as a university we have a Mission Statement, we have a Strategic Plan and beneath that Academic Plans so we know as an institution what our goals are."

Professor Allen encouraged him with a nod. "Agreed, but how does this translate at the subject level?"

"I was getting to that." He risked a wink at the Dean. "It should support the best environment for knowledge production. Help maintain a good research culture where all staff benefit from research group membership. Research leaders will be developing junior staff, getting them cited in the best journals, growing them. Then the subject as a whole needs to ensure the crossover of new knowledge into teaching."

"Easy, isn't it." Professor Allen added.

As he opened his office door the inter-connecting door opened simultaneously. "Sorry David," Lindsay said, "but the Director of HR has been after you all morning and has made Hilary put a working lunch with him in your diary, he was very insistent."

"A working lunch? Any idea what it's about?"

"No, I was hoping you would tell us."

"Guess I'll find out soon, have a seat, just need to check my emails."

He picked his way through his dozen or so unread messages reading those from senior staff first. "Anything happening?" he asked as he read.

"Not a great deal." Lindsay replied, "Professor Stevens popped in looking for you, the Engineers are upset no one believes in their new course proposals. David? I need to speak to you about something."

"Sure" he answered, looking up from a message from the Registrar about a visit from the Chair of University Council. He realised he wasn't really listening when Lindsay changed her mind.

"We can talk later."

"How about after lunch, I haven't got anything important on."

The Director of Human Resources had his office at the very end of the half a floor of the administrative building devoted to his unit on the top floor. In order to get to his office you had to walk past and exchange nods and greetings with at least ten people. Consequently, you could never slip in and out of the suite unseen. If you had been to HR everybody knew you had been there. As he made his way through the throng of people experts he wondered what the meeting was about. Nothing he was involved in required this. Not the outcome of his interview, nor an unlikely re-grading of his job. Which left negative things. Perhaps someone had made a complaint about him or he had fallen out of a shake-up of the Registry. Shelagh would have tipped him off if it were either of those. He had no idea what it could be about. Finally, he reached the desk of the PA to Dr Simon Godfrey and was waved on through an open door, which Dr Godfrey immediately closed behind him.

"Thank you for making the time Mr Leicester. I don't think we have met like this before?" he added, offering his hand. "Please take a seat."

David sat at the end of a long table. Sunlight glared from the windows of what was a large corner office. He felt instantly that he had taken the wrong seat, the one position that took the full energy of the midday sunshine, reddening his face and reducing his vision.

"Actually, help yourself to some lunch over here before we start" the Director said beckoning him over to a side table with a platter of assorted sandwiches and cheeses.

"Same old stuff" he said, "sometimes it's a relief when you are allowed to buy your own lunch." He laughed.

Dr Godfrey was a similar age to David, late thirties. Head hunted from an investment bank by the Vice-Chancellor, or so the rumours claimed. He wasn't sure if his doctorate was honorary. He was a little under six feet but athletic in build, with arms and shoulders that appeared to struggle with the confinement of a suit, his hair had reduced to a thin v shape on the top of his head with sides neatly cut and his bright blue eyes and open smile made it difficult for David to measure him. Dr Godfrey was not a typical university administrator.

"I'm afraid the disembodied voice of the Pro Vice-Chancellor Quality, Professor Lamb will be joining us. We have no choice in that."

"Ok," said David, "You do know I have no idea what this is about, don't you?"

"Yes," replied Dr Godfrey, "I should hope that is the case." He slid a phone across the table and took the opposite seat, pressed the speaker button and tapped in an extension number. "Geoff, hello, I'm here with David Leicester, how do you want to do this?"

"Hello Simon, hello David. I think as I can't see either of you it's probably better if you outline things to David and I'll come in where I need to."

"Ok Geoff, no problem. The first thing we should say is that no one is taking notes here and that nothing that is said here today has any bearing on any actions that follow from this meeting and that you, David, are not a related party, or a witness and that you will not be required to make any statements."

"That's reassuring," he joked uneasily.

"But you will have to be a bit louder when you speak David."

"Sorry Professor Lamb."

Dr Godfrey smiled a genuine-looking smile. "You have a member of staff, Lindsay Parsons. A couple of days ago she contacted me directly by email and I spoke to her away from here. She said she was having a problem with a senior colleague coming on to her and that this person wouldn't take the hint that she wasn't interested. She then forwarded to me some emails which she said were good examples of this behaviour. Having read those we just need some context to try to understand what has happened here. And so, here we are."

"Perhaps," Professor Lamb interrupted, "it should fall to me to say that the colleague under scrutiny here is the Registrar Jonathan Richards and while you might feel this puts you in an awkward position, let me assure you that it doesn't, we are all obliged to examine the issue objectively once it is before us. Naturally, this is all in the strictest confidence, you shouldn't discuss this with anyone but ourselves."

After pausing to be certain that the Pro Vice-Chancellor had finished, Dr Godfrey stood up and lowered the blinds on the sun-drenched window. "If we could start with you telling us a little about Lindsay?"

"Lindsay is a very able member of my team, the best I have," He was struggling to think properly without the opportunity to prepare himself. Here he was chatting cordially with members of the university senior management team about something very serious and being off-the-cuff was not one of his strengths. "She has been in Admissions for nearly two years, she is very capable, articulate, a good organiser, very reliable and has a good career ahead of her."

"Jonathan was on the interview panel for her post?" Asked Dr Godfrey.

"Yes, admittedly she wasn't the strongest candidate on the day but the Registrar vouched for her and he was right, I couldn't have recruited a better person."

"With hindsight," the Director continued "have you ever seen any interaction between them that would now make you feel concerned?"

And here it was. A chance event that comes along only a few times in a person's life in which you can alter circumstance in your favour without penalty, if you are careful. David realised that he had hesitated too long but also that his pause appeared like commendable reticence.

"Nothing clear cut," David began, "I knew from the time of the interview panel that he had an interest in her and that he knew her prior to her joining the Registry. There have been occasions when I've come back into the office and it was just the two of them and their conversation seemed to change. But I didn't really think anything of it, she was often quiet for a time immediately after those encounters."

"Anything else?" Professor Lamb asked.

"There was an odd moment at the last Christmas party", David continued, "it was towards the end of the evening and a certain type of song was playing. Jonathan made a theatrical open armed gesture to her and more or less persuaded her to dance with him. She didn't look comfortable, but we thought it was innocent."

As he walked back to his office he attempted to deal with a mixture of fear and elation. He had taken a risk and his hopes now lay on his comments being nothing more than the right sort of background noise rather than providing anything worth repeating in further conversations. It was still lunchtime and his offices were empty. He checked his email for anything from Professor Allen but there was nothing.

Outside it had started to rain, the yew trees huddled, students and staff walked quickly through the quad and a puddle formed on the flat roof of the student shop. After a time he heard his staff return, laughing at how miserable the weather was and who had ordered the worst meal from the refectory. He opened the interconnecting door and asked Lindsay to join him on the pretext of discussing revised recruitment targets. He asked her to close the door behind her.

"I guess we can have that talk now," David said.

Lindsay, her long brown hair slightly flattened by the rain, studied him for a few seconds before appearing to come to a decision.

"This is not easy."

"No."

"Jonathan's problem was, or is, that he cannot accept that it is over."

"Over" David repeated mechanically.

"He is more than thirty years older than me and look, I'm the mature one."

He felt his career begin to unravel. "But this isn't what you told HR."

"You know about that? No, it isn't," replied Lindsay, "I don't want to destroy his career or his marriage, I just want him to leave me alone."

"Well, his marriage is up to him and his conscience but his career is probably screwed."

"It was harassment David, I want him to stop and he can't."

"Yes, of course, sorry."

"And it isn't like I didn't given him plenty of warnings before I went to Human Resources."

Lindsay looked at him and then down at the table, "So, what happens next? I can't work somewhere where I am hated."

"I don't know Lindsay, I honestly wish I did, but I don't."

David felt unable to work for the remainder of the afternoon. While he knew his contribution to the case against the Registrar was small, he had nevertheless made one and had signed up himself up to the consequences of Lindsay's action. Now he had to wait for all the moving parts to stop. It was after 4pm and still no word from Professor Allen. He was beginning to feel that he wanted the job in Science after all. Tempted to take a rare early finish to the day he decided to see if Shelagh was free. Her detachment was probably what he needed at this moment.

Shelagh was in her office and available.

"I was just going to call you, we need to have a talk."

"Oh. I have no news," said David, "looks like I didn't get it."

"Don't be silly," Shelagh replied. "Andrew will make you wait until 5pm." Shelagh shifted in her seat and said nothing further. Conversations with Shelagh were often like this, a long silence until the point had gone. Not that it was rehearsed, she was not Jonathan Richards, she just did not communicate in the way that most people did.

"Well," She announced, "there will be a full Registry-wide meeting tomorrow at which Jonathan will tell staff that he is taking early retirement and that I will act as Registrar."

"I don't know what to say Shelagh, congratulations!"

"Thank you. That's not why I wanted to see you. I will apply for the post when it is offered, in the meantime I will need someone to cover my areas and act as Senior Assistant Registrar."

As he walked back to his office he knew two things. Lindsay might not escape the rumours that would probably begin soon, but she would have time to find a position elsewhere if she wanted a new start. Secondly, that for a few hours perhaps, Professor Allen would not understand why his offer would be declined.

Inflation

The couple emerged from a restaurant on John Street in Bath to a warm Wednesday evening in the third week of June. She is tall with long straight blonde hair that lingers closely to the contour of her back. The pair walk together, arms occasionally in gentle collision. He is oblivious to his surroundings and sounds as though he is humming as he fidgets with the contents in the pocket of his J Crew Crosby suit jacket. He is about five foot ten with short, thin black hair and neat beard stubble, only slightly taller than the woman. He is overweight but dresses to disguise this. He is not humming though, he is teasing her for the way she thanked their waiter.

Phil Clarke will be forty tomorrow. His wife Leanne, who is three years younger, had arranged a mid-week break in advance of a dinner party at the weekend for friends and some family at their flat in Southwark. "I don't think we can go this way," Leanne said, raising her chin. Ahead of them a blue and white tape cordon fluttered across Quiet Street blocking the route through to their hotel. Two policemen stood in conversation a few yards beyond it. "Are they really carrying guns?" She asked.

They continued down John Street and found their way to The Raven off Queen Street, ordered a real ale and a Mojito and sat at a large wooden table near the door in silence for a while. It was a slow night. "You have to make small talk Clarky," Leanne teased.

"Do I?" he laughed.

"Yes," she answered "and you have to look at me when you do."

Leanne Clarke was a beautiful woman, she had modelled cosmetics after university. A small thin face but with disproportionately large brown eyes, a small mouth. Blondeness arrived after her thirtieth birthday, after the end of a bad relationship.

"How many important conversations do you think you have in a life?"

"Better than climate change as a topic I suppose." She laughed.

"Really though. Less than the fingers of one hand?" He held up a hand and paused, daring her to not be entertained. "Two hands if you have children."

"I don't know Clarky. How about the one where your dad told you the facts of life?" She mimed removing a condom from its wrapper and then putting it over her head.

"Ha! Yes! Or your mother's on personal hygiene." He mimed inverting a shower head as though it were a distasteful act.

Leanne laughed, "maybe the reverse is more true, how many important conversations do you manage to avoid having in a life?"

"Well with that cue," Phil said, getting to his feet, "I'll back in a minute."

Phil Clarke did not feel middle-aged. He had been an investment manager at London City Investments Trust since his early thirties, normally edging his peers on yield. He had none of the advantages of his colleagues, he had built his own wealth taking risks with his own capital knowing that if he failed he would have nothing to fall back on. Now, tonight, after an evening of tapas and too much wine he was as content as he could be. Leanne was stunning, he was so lucky. They owned a large flat in a good part of the city, he owned two Audis and had enough in the bank and in other secure and more speculative positions to retire now if he wanted to.

Back in the lounge Leanne was reading messages on her phone. Nicole had finally bedded the student bartender at her local wine bar. Denise had spent too much on shoes. Although it was the day before a landmark birthday for her husband she had been having bad feelings. She couldn't as yet define them or what they meant but they made her feel unwell. It did not make any sense of course, but dismissing whatever was gathering within her never did work. Phil returned with a second round of drinks.

"When did you last speak to Abby?" Leanne asked.

"Not for a few months." He sighed as he recognised the familiar pattern of the routine before him, to him it seemed that she was about to begin down a path that inevitably led to a fight.

"How many is a few?"

Abby was his nine-year-old daughter from his previous marriage and, as he had given himself completely in an affair with Leanne while still married to her mother, this part of his past he had successfully boxed off as belonging to an earlier, unhappy version of himself.

"Easter I think, when I took her for pizza and chocolate. Look, Leanne, this isn't one of the important conversations, do we have to talk about this now?"

But Leanne was not reassured by his lack of contact with Abby and now, helplessly, she was thinking about her abortion. She knew she couldn't talk about it, it was definitely her decision, he didn't force her. It was his birthday, but she could not suppress her feelings. She had agreed that a termination was the best solution in the year of their affair, a year of passion and anger, a year where they spoke about love and in which there was no space for a new life in such chaos. How much effort had he put into the case against having a baby, it was difficult to think back in a clear way to those discussions, she couldn't easily recreate them, just the pain and then loss and then numbness. She felt herself start to cry and because she knew she couldn't stop and didn't want to upset him she got up and left without saying anything else.

Phil didn't want to chase after her. This was not his fault, he couldn't believe that she had done this to him on his fortieth birthday. He decided to finish his drink.

She stopped outside the fishing tackle shop on Pulteney Bridge when she knew she had gone in the wrong direction for their hotel. It had gone 9:30pm and the city had turned dark, she was conscious of cars flowing past her, luminescent and loud, people glanced into her face as they had to walk around her. She had finished crying now and was beginning to be more conscious of the moment. She checked her phone again and looked behind her for a fourth time but he had not followed, and he had not called her. She brought up a street map and plotted her walk back to the Gainsborough.

Five years ago when she was introduced to Phil by a friend of her brother at a flat party in Canary Wharf she had been intimidated by how magnetic he seemed. He didn't talk about himself though, he wanted to know all about her. School, university, career to date, relationships. With hindsight perhaps it was all about her body, or perhaps he couldn't talk about himself for one big practical reason. And so her understanding of him was never fixed. It wasn't that he was complicated, just that he had been capable of deception. At the time she had been a vocal techniques tutor at Morley College and wallowing in the break-up from a three-year relationship. Her daydreams had extended to a nice apartment and Mediterranean holidays. Yet in five years with Phil her world had rearranged itself beyond any expectation she had ever had. Holidays and wine-soaked sunsets in Milan, Pattaya and Nassau, motorcycling in Bangalore and Crete. He had told her there was no need for her to work as soon as he knew he loved her.

As she approached the hotel she could see him waiting for her. "I'm sorry," she said, "That was very selfish of me."

"I'm just glad you're ok", he replied, putting his arm around her waist, "I think we had too much wine at dinner, we don't do alcohol very well."

He had hoped he was convincing but in reality Phil was still annoyed that she had ruined the evening. "I think we'll give the bar a miss, let's just go to our room, yes?"

"Oh," Leanne answered, "we didn't do the bath. The Thermae bath, that is the unique thing about this hotel."

But Phil had already escorted her to the lift.

They arrived at Codford St Peter at 5am the next morning, a few minutes after sunrise. Leanne in a blue floral sun dress and sandals and Phil in pale blue shirt, trousers and Hugo Boss leather bomber jacket. Both tired and quiet they walked over to the recreation ground where a team of men had unfurled, beyond an upended hamper basket the size of a tractor, the impossible carcass of a hot air balloon which seemed to stretch so far into the distance that the likelihood of it being transformed into a vehicle seemed absurd.

"I'm not sure," Phil began, "whether I am relieved or not that the weather is good enough for this thing to go ahead."

They walked up to a man in a reflective yellow vest and Leanne offered their tickets, "How long before it's ready?" She asked.

"Just a few minutes while we blow some air into her," he replied, "rest of your group's over there." he gestured.

Leanne watched as the men placed a giant fan near the mouth of the envelope and saw the nylon ripple and fall along its great length until the material appeared weightless and could no longer prevent the need to rise. Then the burner gushed hot air. Slowly, very slowly the envelope became a cone and Zeppelin-like. The morning sun glowed through the red skein of the balloon and Leanne felt herself transfixed by the scene. With a few more gusts the balloon began to lift from prone and the ground crew braced to hold it down.

"That basket's not looking so big now," Phil commented, "Come on, the herd is moving."

The sixteen passengers climbed aboard, the pilot, a grey-bearded tall thin man with a mischievous-looking face asked them to steady for the take off and told the ground crew to release. "Looks like we're blowing Amesbury way you lucky lot" he chuckled.

Over the minutes there followed a series of questions from the passengers about altitude, steerage and landing which he answered patiently.

The balloon climbed like a soundless elevator, below they could hear the crew joking, a dog barked. Phil gripped the edge of the gondola and with his other hand reached out to hold Leanne's. He had forgiven her for the abrupt end to their evening, forgiven her for not wanting to make love. She was so beautiful, by far the most attractive woman he had been involved with and now as the balloon drifted over Parsonage Down he realised how fortunate he was to be with such a funny, slim and striking woman. Perhaps they could try again, today was his birthday after all. He let go of the gondola and put his arm around her waist. "Shall we stay on?" He asked, "Try this thermae bath, then maybe the room service?"

Leanne touched his arm reassuringly, "We can't Phil, I have to be at Jane's baby shower tomorrow morning." She looked at his heavy unshaven face, his wrinkled brow and she struggled with her irrational feelings once again, there was something unfamiliar about Phil Clarke and she didn't understood why she felt that way. She surprised herself when she realised that what she was feeling was revulsion. She released his hand to find her sunglasses. The hour had nearly passed when the pilot asked the passengers to look directly forward over the edge of the basket a few miles ahead of them, "there's Stonehenge," he said "I have to look for a landing, sorry we couldn't get closer."

"Listen, can you hear the drums?" The young, shaven-headed man to the right of the pilot asked.

"What's that all about?" Another passenger asked.

"An excuse to smoke weed?" Phil offered.

"Summer Solstice," said the pilot.

And now they could see people around the ancient stones, a festival of sorts, though one of just people and monoliths.

"Before the sunrise you are meant to contemplate the past and the present and after the sun is up you wish the coming harvest well."

The balloon had begun its descent, the yellow stubble of a cropped field rushed towards them. The pilot told the passengers to grip the top of the gondola and bend their knees against the landing but the impact was minor.

Biscuit Tin

It had taken four hours to drive with one break from Junction 23 of the M5 to Pontefract. His early finish on a Friday meant they had arrived mid-evening. He turned off Grove Road before Pease Park into Churchbalk Lane and pulled over to the kerb. There he sat for a moment in his dark blue fifteen-year-old car, son Jack and daughter Becky in the back, wife Sophie alongside him.

"Stop kicking boy, it's getting on my nerves." he snapped.

"Have a toffee love," said Sophie, trying to calm him down.

"Yeah, sorry," he replied. "Not looking forward to this."

Steve Beresford was a 36-year-old production supervisor at Muller in Bridgwater, three years in post and as a result he and his family now had a mortgage on a new build three-bedroom terrace in Kings Down.

"Right, out you get kids." He said. She grabbed his hand, "squeeze back baby."

"Let your dad go first." She called as they swung open their doors and raced up the path to a red brick semi-detached house. Steve took the suitcase from the boot of the car and chased after them. "Wait!" He shouted as the front door was opened by a small, thin older woman with long wavy grey hair wearing a yellow t-Shirt and jeans.

"Hello Di," Steve said putting his hand on her shoulder, "sorry for your loss."

"Hello Steve, kids, Sophie, come on in. Now Jack and Becky, your cousins are in the lounge and there's some biscuits and pop on the table."

The family moved into the hallway.

"Can we see Granddad?" Becky asked.

"Later." Di replied, coaxing her into the lounge.

"And why are all the curtains closed?" Asked Jack.

Steve and Sophie followed Di to the kitchen. It was small but modern, cherry veneer cabinets, orchids on the window ledge beyond the sink basin, and across the faux granite work surfaces stacked cans of beer, stout and lager, a two-thirds full bottle of whisky and some bottles of white wine.

"Where should I put this?" Steve asked, looking down at the suitcase he was dragging behind him.

Di had lit a cigarette and stood with the fingernails of her free hand resting on the breakfast bar. "I thought you'd be staying at the Premier Inn, I'll make up a room, just leave it there for now." She looked at them both for a moment and added, "have you eaten, I could do some sandwiches?"

"No, we're all fine." Steve answered, "We ate at the services."

"Best I smoke this outside with so many children in the house," Di said, "get yourselves a drink then."

Sophie waited for her to leave before whispering "Cow!"

Steve was silent, he poured himself a large whisky and opened the door to the dining room.

When he was a child his dad had owned a caravan. They had a few summer holidays out of it before it pulled the guts out of their hatchback. One year they toured Scotland, another summer was spent just outside of Scarborough and the last was a hot summer bumping their way down the coast of Wales from Aberystwyth to St Davids. His mum had still been alive then. He could remember the three of them walking hand in hand at Porthselau, the hot beach day colours, the sunlight blinding them to all but their silhouettes on the wet sharp sand. Ice cream and happiness.

His dad's coffin lay against the party wall. He had been dressed in a black suit that was too big for him. On the mantelpiece above the gas fire a candle burned, rosemary beads hung from its base. Steve and his father had not been similar in height and build, he was just under six foot, his dad was a good few inches shorter, Steve had to watch his weight, he was broad-shouldered and had a large appetite, his dad was thin and slight. Steve still had a little hair over his crown, his father had none. Now he was no longer pink-faced, without a frown, eyes closed and without any recognizable expression. Sophie took his hand and leant against him.

"Stevie boy! It's been a long time." He turned around to see his brother James marching towards him, a hug extended.

"James." He muttered, returning a couple of the back-slaps.

Di had reappeared with a bottle of wine and whisky in either hand, seeing who needed a top up, "He was a fine man Sam."

"Fireman Sam." James said quietly before nudging Steve. "I've got a bit of coke if it'll help."

"You're alright James, we're good thanks."

"Sixty-one though," said Sophie, "It's nothing."

"Bugger wouldn't stop smoking would he," James replied, "isn't that right mum, a chain smoker like you."

"I'm ignoring that, I'm going to sort out a room for your brother." Di laughed. She put her cigarette packet and lighter on the breakfast bar and gave James a look before going upstairs.

"Where's Maxie? Is she in the other room?" asked Steve taking a seat at the dining table.

James looked away. "We're on a break I suppose."

"Again!" Sophie laughed. "Are the boys with you?"

"Yeah, in the other room, we're all living here at the minute, yours are growing up fast, eight and ten?"

"seven and nine" Said Sophie, "talking of which, we should get them in here then up to bed without scaring the hell out of them, you two go in the kitchen."

When he was a young teenager his parents accepted that he would never get out of bed in time for morning Mass and so let him go alone in the evening. He never went of course, he would just go around to a friend's house, smoke cigarettes and listen to music. He couldn't remember the exact age he stopped believing but remembered how scared he was of death, it had been crammed into him. The soul could not transcend without Christ's intercession and the love of God, there was only death and nothingness outside of the church and if you walked away God would turn his back and never think of you again. But it was all meaningless nonsense. And when God had not struck him down for thinking that he had just got on with his life.

"What time's the priest coming round?" Steve asked, pouring himself another large whisky.

"Father Mac has been and gone, busy man in all this hot weather."

They waved to the four children as they walked quietly in single file into the dining room, Di and Sophie following.

He looked at James, a tall, thin man a few years younger than himself with cropped hair and with a lot more ink on his arms and neck than his own pair of tattoo sleeves. He looked at his red nostrils, his pockmarked cheeks and thought how ill he looked.

"Nice photographs of the old man with Di, couple of you and him as well." Steve said gesturing to the wall space behind the kitchen door.

"He was a good bloke," James replied, opening a can of lager, "you should have come up here more often. Been over five years since I've seen you."

"Night, kids!" they shouted as the procession returned and headed back down the hall for the stairs.

"So, are you working?" Steve asked.

James paused "I get by."

"Di helps."

"Yeah, mum helps."

"So, what did you do to Maxie?"

"Not me mate, there's this bloke at her work she can't stay away from, she might go too far this time."

"She's always forgiven you when you've messed up."

"Yeah, but now she thinks she doesn't love me."

They sat drinking in silence for a while. Upstairs they could hear Di and Sophie saying goodnight to the children.

"How are things with you and Sophie?"

"Phenomenal mate. She's everything I need."

"What's she doing now work wise?"

"She's a teaching assistant at the local school."

"That sounds about right." James replied.

Di and Sophie returned to the kitchen talking about the stiff window in the guest bedroom which would need two hands to close if it got chilly in the night. Di made sure they all had drinks before leading them back into the dining room and then abandoning them in order to have a cigarette in the back garden.

"Do I say goodbye now?" Sophie asked, looking at Sam.

"There'll be time in the morning before the undertaker arrives," James said.

"Are you sitting up with him?" Steve asked his brother.

"Not me, no, mum will though."

Di reappeared smelling of tobacco. "I should probably do this now," she said, holding out her closed fist to Steve, "it's Sam's wedding band from when he was with your mum." Steve felt the tiny thing drop cold on his palm, he pressed it into his hand with his fingertips.

"He didn't leave a will you know, your dad, I know you're not wondering, you can see we're not rich."

"I know that Di, I haven't wondered." He looked through the door to the coffin.

"For my fiftieth," Di said, "he took us to Tenerife. Daft bugger couldn't afford it and didn't tell me about the credit card until we got back, but I'll always remember him trying to sing like Sinatra. Yeah, he did Summer Wind on karaoke night and his dancing, God he couldn't dance."

"I remember on my sixteenth birthday," said Steve, "he gave me a packet of cigarettes and said you're a man now so no more sneaking behind my back. Then he asked me to smoke one standing in front of him, he asked me if I enjoyed it. He said I could smoke in the garden after that."

"Let's toast the old man then," James suggested, "a good dad and husband!"

"Amen." Steve said softly, moving closer to the coffin. "Night dad," he said, "I'll see you before you go." He stood on the spot as the room began to slowly spin. Sophie took the glass from his hand, put it on the table and led him out of the dining room. "Night all, see you in the morning."

"Night love!" Said Di

"Night Stevie boy!" James called.

They made their way to his childhood bedroom, conscious of Jack and Becky sleeping on an airbed on the floor, Sophie made Steve pause at the door while she picked her way carefully across the room to put the bedside light on. She helped him out of his clothes and into bed. "I wanted to stay up all night with him you know." Steve mumbled. "You are in no state," she replied "and I don't think your dad would be offended."

"I love you," he said.

"I know you do."

He looked at Sophie, her long brunette hair, green-blue eyes and warm smile. "I love it when you do the sentimental drunk thing," she said before kissing him fully on the mouth, "except for the snoring bit, that's not so lovely."

"I'm always aroused when we're alone together."

"I know."

"Check."

"I don't want to check."

"You see that hatch up there?" Steve said. "I used to keep my secret stash up there as a kid."

"Your porn?"

"Cigarettes, dope, the lot, in a biscuit tin behind the water tank. It's probably still there."

The next morning things happened quickly, his family were showered, dressed in their best clothes and fed just before the undertakers arrived, sealed the coffin and ushered the household to their cars. Steve had meant to sit with his father for a few minutes alone but never got the opportunity. It was a bright Saturday morning in early July. They drove slowly through the town, the market stalls were out for the Liquorice Festival and Southgate heaved with families. They drove on, up Jubilee way and off to St Joseph Church. Di and James travelled in the limousine, Steve, Sophie and the children in his car.

"Can we go to town dad, after church?" Asked Jack excitedly.

"Not today boy, we have to say goodbye to granddad."

"Not fair," Jack said to Becky, "didn't even know granddad very much."

"Enough!" Sophie snapped.

They parked and in their hurry to catch up with Di and James walked by the priest standing to the left of the church door smoking a cigar.

"Steven, It's been years."

"Father Mac." Steve replied reluctantly shaking the offered hand of a large chubby man with short, neat grey hair and oversized black spectacles.

"A sad day and a happy day. All the usual symmetries of The Faith. No comfort and all you'll ever need etcetera."

"Yes I suppose so, Father."

"Is this your family then, Steven? Ah beautiful. The children are too," he laughed as he shook Sophie's hand and deliberately patted the heads of Jack and Becky.

"It's a big turnout for him Father, I wasn't sure what to expect."

"He had a lot of friends up at the factory in Featherstone, I think many have come down for a big send off. Talking of which and all that, I'll catch up with you again for a drink or two, and don't feel like an outsider, you're his boy." He tapped out his cigar and stuffed it in a case which then disappeared beneath his surplice.

Feeling awkward in his black suit, Steve led his family toward the pews near the altar, then slid into the second one behind Di, James and his dad's surviving brother Joe, Aunty Viv and their three sons and wives and all of the children. Everybody mouthed greetings and smiled and nodded.

The congregation then began to sing a hymn but Steve didn't join in. He watched but didn't really listen as uncle Joe, Di and James read the Bidding prayers and told tales of his father, memories that were not his. At points Sophie held his hand and when it was time to leave and continue at the grave-side he found himself content to lag a little behind the other mourners and not hustle for a place near the interment.

The blessings complete they made their way back to the house.

"Come into the lounge Steve," Di insisted. "Are you drinking?"

"I have to drive later."

"Fair enough. Sit down next to me. I wanted you to have something else and to show you I'm not some sort of callous woman who made him throw these things away."

The lounge was full of people, some like Joe and his family he knew but many he had never seen before. His children were playing in the back garden, Sophie had brought the water pistols in addition to their other toys and he thought the sound of laughing children was a good noise to have at a wake.

Di, in her navy-blue jacket and cream blouse, her long grey hair tied neatly back handed him an old red vinyl-covered photograph album. "It's you, your mum and Sam."

Di took a large sip of her drink. "Do you remember when we met for the first time? You were seventeen. We met at the racecourse for a picnic, you with your dad, me with James. Do you remember how angry you were with your dad? For tricking you, you thought."

"I remember."

"He thought about you all the time. I hope we can stay in touch, I will always be able to talk about your dad." Di patted his knee, scooped up her cigarettes and lighter and left the room. Sophie slid down next to him. He guessed that it was around that time, the picnic, that he started to turn his back on his father.

"Thought she'd given up smoking the length of time it took her to move her backside." She said, slipping her arm through his.

"I think we should go soon, I've had enough."

Sophie leant over and whispered, "suitcase is packed."

"I'll get our stuff and load the car, you go play with the kids, you don't have to sit in here."

Nothing of his childhood remained in the bedroom now, furniture, carpet, curtains, even the wallpaper was different. It had changed so much it was difficult to imagine a younger version of himself in it. He had a single bed, not a double and it wasn't facing the window in the centre of the room. His carpet had been navy blue, this was beige with a brown rug. He had a free-standing wardrobe, a desk and chair, now there was a built-in wall of cupboards with full-length mirrors, two bedside tables and a small dressing table and chair. He sat on the bed and opened the album Di had given him. It began with photographs of his mum and dad as a young couple then with him as baby and progressively older until teenage and half attempting to be out of shot. There were very few of his mum and she didn't look how he remembered her. He had an image of a tall, friendly and flirtatious woman with long blonde hair, a woman who drew attention. The woman in these photographs seemed awkward and reluctant, even a little embarrassed. She had been gone for twenty years and there was too much he didn't know and would now never know. The conversations he should have had but had been to angry with the world and his father to have them.

Sitting on the bed he looked up at the ceiling, at the access to the roof space in the corner and for no reason other than it summoned a real memory of childhood, he took the chair, set it against the wall, stepped up and lifted and slid the panel across the beams. He felt around with his right hand and nearly laughed when he felt tin. Oddly, there was something in the box, it certainly had weight. He pulled it out of the space and down to chest level expecting to see when he opened it a familiar magazine or two but it wasn't magazines it was money. Ten stacks of fifty twenty-pound notes, each held together with a thick and wide blue elastic band. He looked closely at one of the bands, indented in its centre were the words Linpac, Featherstone UK. Outside he could hear bird song and beneath that, the sound of his children playing without care. He opened his suitcase and tipped the money in.

Downstairs in the kitchen James grabbed his arm as he tried to get to the garden, he seemed drunk or high. "Could I have a quick word mate." he said, his sweating face a little too close to Steve's. "No problem," he replied setting the suitcase down. "What is it?"

James moved between him and the door, "I hate to ask, but with everything that's happened, Maxie, Sam and all, I'm in a bit of a mess, could you lend us some cash, I've got school uniforms and stuff to get."

"Let's go outside," Steve suggested, picking up the suitcase again. "I've got about two hundred in my wallet, you can have that, it's not a loan, will that help?"

James just nodded and took the cash. "I love you brother." He said patting Steve's shoulder.

"We're getting off in a few minutes, it's a long drive, it's been good to see you again, maybe you can come down to the South West?"

"Yeah sure, I'd like that." Though they both knew that this wouldn't happen.

"Soph!" Steve shouted and then waved his wife and children towards him from where they sat on a bench at the end of the garden.

"I'm going to go back in," James said.

"Ok, look after yourself mate," They shook hands firmly. "We'll be in to say goodbye in a minute."

Sophie in her simple black dress, her eyes fixed on his and a wonderful smile on her face, walked up and kissed him.

"Let's get out of here." Steve whispered. "Becky, Jack, go into the front room, give Di a kiss, say goodbye to her and I want you to say sorry about granddad, ok?"

"Nearly over babe" Sophie said putting an arm around his waist.

They walked quickly through to the lounge, Steve hauling the suitcase with him, he stood it against the front door. Then went back and tackled the room. He shook uncle Joe's hand, waved to aunty Viv, smiled at his cousins whose names he wasn't too sure about. Father Mac stood up from his seat next to Di. He put an arm on his shoulder and steered him around so that they both had their backs to the room.

"I don't suppose we'll be seeing you again Steven."

"Well I'll probably…"

"It doesn't matter lad, there'd be nothing here for me but bones too."

"I suppose not." He replied, wishing he was already in the car.

"You have made yourself a great looking family of your own. And, you came from a great family too. If only these bodies of ours weren't so fragile eh? Do you know what Ponte's motto is? I mean, do you remember what it is?"

Di was talking excitedly to another woman he did not recognise, ripples of smoke rising from her wrinkled hand, her garden smoking rule having long since lapsed.

"Post mortem patris pro filio."

"Yeah, I know, after the death of the father support the son. One of the few things I do remember from St Wilfreds."

"Your dad was a good man, a kind man. He didn't drink or gamble, he ignored the flaws in people and he went out of his way to help them. Drove the minibus for me most weekends you know. An example any son could follow, yes?"

"Yes Father."

"He just got on with living after Pat died. Didn't have a bad word to say about your absence. Proud of you he was."

"I know, Father."

"Goodbye Di," he heard Sophie say, and beneath her voice Jack and Becky wondering aloud what a liquorice festival was.

A strong smell of nicotine surrounded him and Di was pulling him away from the priest, "Ok Father, enough now, leave the man alone and get yourself another drink."

Steve and Father Mac smiled at each other. "Goodbye lad."

"Goodbye Father."

Di was still holding onto his arm. "You're off then, I hope the journey is ok."

"I wanted to thank you Di, before we left." He began, "we've never really spoken much and I wanted to thank you. My dad loved you a lot and I need to thank you for that."

"He was an easy man to love."

He noticed her eyes were beginning to tear up again and so he hurried his family out of the house. He couldn't see James in the lounge but said a general goodbye to all and followed Sophie and the children out to the car. Di stood for a moment on the doorstep and waited for them all to wave after they had climbed into the car before closing the front door for a final time.

"Do you mind if I go the cemetery before we head off, I'll drop you and the kids off in town, they can look at the stalls."

"Of course, are you ok baby?"

"Yeah. I want to say goodbye to them both. Mum and dad."

"Do you want me to come?"

"No, it's ok." He looked in the rear-view mirror. "He gave me something you know."

"Your dad?"

"Yeah. I should have made more of an effort."

"I think he probably understood. Step families eh? You know all about mine."

"Di gave me a photo album too, didn't even recognise mum. It was her but not how I remembered her. Anyway, the thing he left me, we need to talk about it later, because I decided he left it for me."

The car turned onto Grove Road, the sun broke through cloud, and heat descended so quickly that both adults lowered their windows. Sophie grabbed his hand after a gear change, groaned when he let go to change again and laughed in triumph when she was able to grab it again. As the car drove on Steve was laughing as Jack was telling Becky how to spell liquorice, incorrectly. Sophie was trying to tune the radio to any song she could sing along to and though they had a number of hours of driving ahead of them and would have to stop several times for food and toilet breaks, they had all begun to feel they were nearly home.

The Blessing of Children

On their first date at La Belle Cochon de Lait in Gravesend Mike and Jennifer talked about still wanting to find the Real Thing. They also spoke about food, parenthood, property, marriage and all the usual things people talk about over restaurant meals, but it was their mutual hunger for love that they both remembered the next day. Jennifer Soames was fifty-three, a divorced mother of two sons, a former schoolteacher now working from her home in Shorne. Mike Lynch was fifty-five, a divorced father of one daughter, a former Housing Manager with Gravesham Borough Council, who currently worked in the bakery section of a supermarket and lived in a small rented one bedroom flat in Northfleet. She discovered that he had quit his job and gone travelling for a time after he knew his divorce was finalised. Over the past few years he had begun to supplement his poor wage by buying and selling rare books and ephemera online.

On their second date they had spent an autumn Saturday mooching around Canterbury. Mike had told her that he was a member of the Communist Party of Britain, not an activist, just someone who paid a monthly subscription because he thought utopian ideas needed to be kept alive. Jennifer confessed to an affair with the father of one her pupils while she was still married. Over coffee in Nasons they discussed why so many curse words focused on genitalia and whether these were more shocking than racist terms. Mike learnt that her sons did not approve of them as a potential couple as he no longer owned his own place. He joked that once he had made her fall in love with him he would force her to sell her house and spend the money on things that would really annoy them. Jennifer said Mike reminded her of a badly built snowman but with better looks and less weight. As they left the department store Jennifer had pretended that she was going to steal a handbag.

The third time they met they had sex. They had talked about sex when they messaged each other but not face to face. They agreed that their best experiences had been spontaneous. Times where they had given in to impulse in the open air. So, the following Saturday they planned a circular walk from Snodland taking in parts of both the Pilgrim's Way and the North Downs Way. As it had been a dry summer finding a suitable place to leave the road from Birling to the Tree Garden to have their picnic was straightforward. They had both spotted a grassy dip of land behind a pair of ash trees. It was not awkward. They had kissed and caressed and after he had come he asked her to show him how to touch her until she had come too.

Now they began to meet more often. They stayed at his flat on the following Tuesday and while she tried not to show what she thought of his place, some pieces like the orange and black striped second-hand sofa, reminded her of life as a student. But it didn't matter because she was falling in love with him. He told her about how his ex-wife had been honest about meeting someone else, and the day she told him that she no longer loved him and wanted to be with her new man. On Thursday they stayed at her house in Shorne and he remembered the quality of life he had lost when he was rejected by Susan. He told her he was falling in love with her and she told him that she had begun to feel the same. He noticed Jennifer didn't like talking about her ex-husband, other than to explain that not only was she mortgage free but that he had also been ordered to pay a large sum to provide for pension and other costs.

The weeks passed. On a Saturday in late November Jennifer drove them to Thetford in Norfolk to meet his daughter Laura and her husband. Both in their early thirties they lived in a detached house on Foxglove Road near the river. Laura's husband Robert was a GP at the Grove Surgery. Laura had recently left her role as an IT analyst at Baxter Healthcare because she was expecting their first child. They were half an hour early.

"Look at you!" Mike exclaimed as his daughter opened the door to them, her stomach large and tight in a red t-shirt, her long brown hair tied back neatly and small round face made up discreetly.

"Dad!" she said giving him a big hug, "and this is Jennifer! You were right, she is so out of your league." The women considered each other. Jennifer was about five foot seven, with shoulder-length brown hair, an oval face with grey-blue eyes and small soft features. She was effortlessly younger looking than her age, dressed in tight casual jeans, fashionable boots and a white boat-neck mohair jumper. Ushered through to the lounge, Mike introduced Jennifer to Robert. The men spoke about Robert's interest in mountain biking and running and Jennifer and Laura talked about Mike.

Laura had cooked a vegetarian pasta for lunch, served with warm poppy seed rolls and home-made lemonade. The four sat at the dining table overlooking the patio and garden. "So, dad says you met on the internet? What was that like?"

"Scary, neither of us had been told that you are meant to lie in your profile."

"But still, how did you find each other?" Laura asked, "I mean, how do you filter people out?"

Mike laughed, "I knew straight away, I had to hope she'd reply."

"I nearly didn't. I think you can see things in photographs of men that women are good at hiding and in how they talk about themselves." Jennifer said, leaning over to kiss him on the cheek.

"Whoah!" Laura laughed, "not at the table!"

"So, what attracted you to my Dad then, Jennifer?"

"You mean apart from the tall, dark, handsome thing he has going on? His kindness I suppose. He's calm, a bit of a thinker. I was looking for that, I suppose. Was he a good dad?"

"Yes, he was a good dad. He has a big heart, always there whether you needed him or not," Laura laughed.

"What do you do for work Jennifer?" Asked Robert making an effort to get into the conversation.

"I teach privately. From home." She replied, "Mostly piano but some mathematics, especially before the exams."

"I wish I could work from home." Robert smiled, "but people refuse to stay well for long enough."

"You've fallen on your feet dad."

After lunch they took a walk in Thetford forest. Robert spent the time talking about diagnostics and diet for avoiding later life diabetes, Laura about her hopes for her unborn boy. Mike and Jennifer walked hand in hand, the late autumn sun gently blinding them all as it appeared to strobe between the trunks of the beech and walnut trees. "I love you." Mike said.

"I know."

As the month drew to an end they had to plan the Christmas holidays. Last year Mike had been alone as Susan and her boyfriend had stayed in Thetford so he had worked all but Christmas Day itself. This year he had put in his request early. Jennifer would normally have her sons and their wives. They agreed that it would be a good idea to have a little get together the fortnight before Christmas in order to avoid making the experience more stressful than it needed to be. For many weeks now they had alternated between sleeping in Shorne and Gravesend. When Mike was on a late shift it was easier for them to stay at his flat. On the whole this had worked well, Jennifer was able to adjust her diary so that they could have time together. They grew closer. They found that they rarely watched television now, they spent evenings with a bottle of wine and just talked. They took turns picking events from their lives and explaining how these moments changed the way they thought. Jennifer regretted not having a daughter and felt guilty that most of her daydreams about what it was going to be like as a mother were based around how to build a lifelong friendship with a girl of her own. Mike admitted that Susan had never really wanted children and that it took everything he had to persuade her to have Laura. He asked Jennifer to marry him and she said yes. The next fortnight passed quickly and the day he was to meet her sons and their wives soon arrived.

For their meal in Shorne they decided on a takeaway so that they could entertain as a team. Mike was setting up the patio heaters either side of a long teak dining table and glancing at his watch too frequently. Richard and Lucinda were first to arrive, Jennifer brought them through to the garden.

"Mike is it? You're a big fella." Richard said as they shook hands, "This is Lu,"

"Nice to meet you Mike, we've both heard a lot about you," said Lucinda, offering a gripless handshake.

"None of it good, mate." Richard added, "What! I'm joking" he said to Lucinda after she elbowed him. Jennifer hadn't finished setting the table so went to get drinks and glasses from the kitchen while the others took their seats. Mike sat facing the young couple. Richard Soames was short and broad, clipped blonde hair, a little flat nose and small blue eyes, a sales manager with a car accessories firm based in Croydon. Lucinda was also short and muscular, thin-faced but warm and talkative, with long black hair and wearing a pale blue sun dress. She helped manage her mother's boutique maternity and baby clothes shop in Maidstone and the couple lived in a large semi-detached house in Sevenoaks. Richard told Mike that he was glad his mum had met someone because she had been alone for a few years and he was beginning to get worried about her.

Jennifer returned with drinks, "I like your dress Lucinda, gorgeous."

The door-bell rang, and Jennifer thinking it was their Chinese meal sent Mike to fetch it. Mike opened the door to Paul and Julie. Paul a tall man of similar height and build to himself who gave him a quizzical look, "Wrong house?" Then laughed in a committed but routine manner.

"We thought dinner had arrived, I'm the Mike you are coming to meet." He invited them in and followed them through to the garden.

Paul chose the seat where Mike had been sitting and Julie sat down alongside him. He nodded to his brother and sister-in-law, "Evening Soames."

Paul was an assistant manager at a large DIY store on the outskirts of Gravesend, he was a tall, overweight man in his early thirties who looked older, his full dark brown hair was cut short and flat, his face was red and dry, his large nose dominated his face. Julie was very petite in contrast, almost girl-like in her blue jeans and pink t-shirt and braided blonde hair, she worked as a courier driver for a parcel company.

The door-bell chimed its three ascending notes again and Jennifer sent Mike off into the house.

"Ok family" Jennifer said looking around the table, "be nice."

Mike returned with two carrier bags of Chinese food and they ate and chatted until they had finished.

Since Jennifer accepted his proposal they had discussed future plans in detail. Jennifer had decided earlier that day that she wanted to make them public. "There is something that I need to say before you are all back here on Christmas day." Mike turned to look at her in surprise, uncertain what she was going to say. Jennifer took his hand. "Mike and I want to be together, so I will be putting the house on the market in January."

"Where are you going then?" Lucinda asked, "Spain?"

"World cruise?" Julie suggested.

"We're going to get a house together, maybe closer to Canterbury." Jennifer replied.

Paul and Richard looked at each other and then at Mike before Richard asked. "You don't mind me asking, mate, could you get a mortgage off what you earn from a supermarket?"

Jennifer leaned between them until she had got Richard's attention, "I will be buying our new place." Richard looked at Paul and sat forward, "This is all a bit quick don't you think? Are you really sure you're ready for such a big step?"

"I'm not negotiating with you Richard."

Mike's free hand began to clench. "I'd be just as happy if she moved into my flat in Northfleet."

"I like Northfleet, sort of quaint." Said Lucinda.

The evening deflated into coffee, mints and polite conversation about television programmes, and the subject of the house was not mentioned again.

After everyone had left and Jennifer had noticed Richard and Paul speaking outside, the couple returned to the kitchen to wash the dishes and glasses.

"Well that was a bit of a shock." Mike said, "I thought you were going to announce our engagement."

"Men are weird about possessions, like it's part of their masculinity," Jennifer replied, "they would have just said stuff behind your back anyway whichever way they'd found out. They'll come around in the end."

Because it was not soluble Jennifer turned the radio on. Outside, a slight breeze had started to ruffle the edges of the tablecloth and the patio heaters glowed amber in the darkness.

"Three things I love about you."

"Five." She replied

"Damn. Ok."

"They have to be better than last time."

"I love you."

"You changed the subject."

Assisted Living

Four years ago Evie Barnes and her boyfriend Matt had taken the bus from Penrith, where she had grown up, along the A66 past Keswick, Bassenthwaite and Cockermouth and down the A596 to the marina-embellished former coal port of Whitehaven. They had enough saved for a deposit and one month's rent. She had a job arranged at The White Swan and it was an exciting time, anything could have happened. But it didn't. Now she was peeling potatoes and talking quietly over a radio newsreader to Jilly, a former senior hospital nurse and assistant manager of Seascale House. Outside, trails of unraked, browned and curled mountain ash leaves which lay in detached groups on the small overgrown lawn revealed themselves as the morning fog finally lifts. Evie, the younger and shorter of the two, sipped her coffee. The pair looked as though they were doing everything with a deliberate slowness. The six residents had all been washed and dressed. Breakfasts of cereal and toast had been eaten and dishes cleared and the three folk that do not prefer to stay in their rooms were now drinking tea and watching morning television in the lounge.

Evie and Matt had lived in the same one-bed flat on Coach Road near the supermarket since moving to the town. She was twenty-three now and a few months ago had been awarded a level three national vocational qualification in adult care. She had planned to work in hospitality since her brief academic hiatus post-school in Penrith where she had worked in the kitchen at Dockray. But the manager at The White Swan was a pervert and she had decided to switch to the care sector. She had already worked at two other Bright Water care homes in Whitehaven before being moved to Seascale.

"She has always stuck to the same version of events." Evie said, rinsing off her dark thumb prints on the last of the potatoes, "but it only makes sense to me if what really happened is the opposite."

"What does Matt think?" Jilly asked as she prepared the chicken for the oven.

Evie laughed gently. "That if my mum had an affair with a married man then I'm just a sperm donation anyway."

"Useful to have the male perspective isn't it?" Jilly teased.

"He has a daughter about the same age as me, she looks like me."

"So, what are you going to do?"

"I don't know. He hasn't replied to the message I sent him last week. So, I don't know."

Jilly wrapped the roasting tray and chicken with foil and slid it into the oven. "Ok pet, if you start on the rooms, I'll finish up here. And see if you can get Beryl to part with some of her newspapers."

Seascale House was actually a six-bedroom bungalow, three bedrooms off each side of the long hall which extended from the lounge/diner. Each room had an ensuite shower room and there was an additional bathroom at the end of the hall which periodically became a store room until Martina, the owner, noticed and complained about its change of use. The room would then be functional for a week or two until the fact that it was never used attracted back all the same bits of furniture and equipment. Room one, end left of corridor was home to Caitlin Ford, an eighty-three-year-old with late stage dementia who spent day and night in foetal positions on her bed. Such was her rigidity that she could easily be bruised after a bed bath, sometimes she would call Evie "mother" or ask her, "who is that man outside the window" there was never conversation as such, just reassurance to Caitlin when she yelped as Evie tried to move her around her bed. Jilly would often say Martina was wrong to allow people who needed such a level of care to be at Seascale, it was unfair on the other residents. Caitlin's son Daniel visited every day for at least an hour. "Would you like some more tea Caitlin?" Evie asked, offering her the lime green beaker. Caitlin smiled and opened her mouth for the straw. Evie quickly hoovered the beige carpet and moved on to the toilet and shower room. She sprayed the sink with disinfectant and wiped the bowl. Her period was five weeks late now, she stood up on her toes to look at her stomach through her slim-fit red pullover and imagined a bulge. She had been putting off buying a test kit, they were so expensive. Room three was Brian Tate, seventy-nine, a tall, moody, thin man who, Jilly said, used to do some form of management work at the Carlisle Royal Mail sorting office. He had suffered a stroke three years ago and used a cane for his left leg after fighting his way out of a wheelchair with the assistance of physiotherapy. He was solitary and stayed away from the Resident's Lounge due to television and, he argued, the infinite repetition of the same conversations. "I was going to clean up, Brian." Evie suggested, knowing he would take the hoover from her and do it himself. In the little over three months she had worked in the home she had never known Brian to have family or friends visit. Beryl Ross was the occupant of Room Four, at eighty-seven the oldest resident at Seascale. Day time routines were much easier with Beryl. Once she had been argued into having her shower which she insisted on sitting through, had been dressed and assisted back to her armchair she just needed a supply of drinks between meals. Most days she would promise to leave something in her will for Evie, tell her that her family had stolen from her and that she once had a fine house in Frizington. Her youngest daughter Megan visited most Saturdays. Evening shifts however, contained a lengthy routine. There was something too wilful about her urinary incontinence, the plethora of night-time drinks, the arrangement of three pads beneath her buttocks rather than wearing just the one, her need to be positioned semi-propped up in bed by two pillows and then the order in which the blankets were laid across her legs and waist. "More tea Beryl? How about your lemon barley, more of that?" Evie asked.

"That's right dear," Beryl replied with a grin.

Evie gave the shower room a quick check, wiped the sink with a cloth and poured some bleach into the toilet pan. Then she tackled the bed, bagging the heavy pads. The blankets were dry but needed washing, she took the bed sheet and the mattress protector. She could do with a new mattress, Evie thought, before getting the air freshener from the shower room and spraying it above their heads.

In the kitchen Jilly was going through files at the table. "Do you think Brian has been struggling with his walking recently?"

"I haven't noticed it," Evie said, "seriously though, how could you tell?"

Jilly laughed, "I think he is, he just doesn't want us to know. I'm trying to find the last time the physio treated him." Evie piled the bedding into the laundry skip in the utility room near the kitchen door and made Beryl her drinks. "Has Brian ever been on anti-depressants?" She asked.

"He wouldn't accept that sort of diagnosis, probably explain to the doctor that watching his life's capital disappear into Martina's bank account month by month would make anyone ill."

"He has his history books."

"Yes, and a good range of mints."

Beryl was reading the Daily Mail when Evie returned with her drinks. Weak sunlight from her window glinted on her glasses. She noticed that she had forgotten to brush the thin patches of her silver-grey hair. "Beryl, I've been asked to see if I can de-clutter your room a bit. Maybe get rid of the newspapers that you've finished with?"

"Eh?" Beryl rasped nasally, "I'm still reading them dear. They're mine. Lot's of good stuff I haven't read yet."

"I know Beryl, but you do have a pile each side of your armchair, it's too many." Evie gestured at the chaotic stacks of dog-eared pages. Knowing she did not have time to follow through with her offer now she added, "how about I take half away after lunch? You can decide which to keep." As she spoke and looked into the sun it occurred to her that she could do more or less do anything, sing, talk in another language and as it would be outside of one of Beryl's routines it would pass unnoticed.

"That's right dear," Beryl mumbled and Evie left her room. Noticing that Brian had put the hoover outside of his closed door, she picked it up and went back to the kitchen.

"How's Matt's job going?"

"He still hates it. I don't think customer service is a strength of his, don't know how he passed an interview for a call centre."

"Well, there isn't much out there and nothing that pays well." Jilly looked up from a magazine, "Beryl is not going to give in without a fight?"

"Something like that."

"You know what we need to do now," Jilly said smirking, "we need to make some scones or a sponge cake for this afternoon."

"You mean me, don't you?" Evie said resignedly.

"We have to be able offer everyone something during the entertainment."

"I should have bought something." She replied, watching Jilly edging closer to the door.

"I'm going to go chat in the lounge for a bit, part of the job you know, socialising."

Evie took out the mixing bowl from the cupboards behind the kitchen table, assembled scales, butter, sugar, eggs, self-raising flour and a small bottle of vanilla essence which had passed its use by date. Matt would say they could not afford a baby yet and he was right, she thought, they could barely afford rent and credit card payments as it was. Either they would both have to be promoted rapidly through their jobs or they would have to go on a waiting list for a housing association place. She felt guilty that all she could see were problems. Perhaps he might react differently though, perhaps. Metal spoon she remembered, not a wooden one. She wiped her eyes. She checked her mobile phone, five minutes to midday, no messages. Her shift was nearly half-way through.

Sunday dinner at Seascale House was served according to how the residents chose to live, Brian and Beryl took their meals on a tray in their rooms and Caitlin was spoon-fed by a carer or sometimes her son, the remaining residents made use of the dining table.

In the Resident's Lounge the long pine table was dressed with floral place mats, a jug each of water and orange squash and a bottle of cheap red wine. Plates for a Sunday dinner were usually arranged in the kitchen to avoid the clutter and additional washing of serving bowls, which meant some minor to and fro over likes and dislikes in advance of serving.

Jilly played chef, her large strong arms fussing above the three plates. "How many roast potatoes should I put aside for you love?"

"Nothing for me today, Matt is driving us up to Penrith to have dinner with my mum."

"Ok, give the gravy a stir and pour it into the boat by the kettle. This one on the right is for Tom when you're ready. I'll go help him move."

The residents took their seats at the table. Jilly helped Tom move from his seat on the sofa into his wheelchair, he then propelled himself to his usual position at the head of table, being the only male, a fact remarked upon with amusement at the same time every day. Tom Waterstone was a small plump bald-headed man of about five foot eight inches, seventy-three, found prone six months ago in his squalid two room flat after an alert to the police by a neighbour who heard the fall. He had suffered a minor stroke and had lost the use of his right leg but behaved as though he had no strength in either. The hospital-appointed physiotherapist had concluded that Mr Waterstone displayed little interest or motivation to recover any independent mobility. Tom adjusted his glasses and thanked Evie for serving him. To Tom's left was Mrs Hill and to his right Mrs Calderdale. All the residents of Seascale had outlived their partners. Perhaps, Evie thought, the sociable three had been alone the longest. She didn't know, they never talked about husbands and wives. They talked about their children often but never their partners.

Jilly brought the other plates. Mrs Calderdale asked who was on shift for the evening as she would need someone to help tie up her hair because her fingers were no longer as precise as they used to be. Evie didn't know a great deal about Elaine Calderdale, she looked in her early to mid-seventies, about five foot seven as she was the same height as her, she had lived on a farm but she wasn't sure what happened after her husband had died. She kept her hair brown and shoulder-length and was quite heavy from the waist down.

"Elenuta this afternoon and overnight," Jilly replied pouring orange squash for her, "Josh in the morning, me in the afternoon."

"Would you like some water Lou?" Evie asked Mrs Hill, resisting an urge to ask her if she felt tired. She had a face that looked tired. Deep lines to the forehead and excess skin had gathered beneath her eyes, a lifetime heavy smoker who had quit after decades of the habit. She had lived most of her life a few miles up the coast in Workington, and Evie knew that she had done a variety of factory and retail jobs as Lou could give her detail on who were the best and worst employers in the town. In fact one of her first questions on being introduced to Evie was about the Bright Water pay rates, which she thought disgusting in comparison to the monthly charge for a room in the bungalow.

"Yes love and a drop of something in it, if you have it."

"Well, you know we have it Lou." Jilly replied, "I'll fetch the gin."

"Glass of wine Tom?" Evie asked, already pouring as he nodded. "Right, think that's everything, enjoy your dinner."

The residents thanked Evie and began to eat their meal. She hurried back to the kitchen, Jilly passed with a bottle of gin and pointing at two meals on separate trays said "Brian's and Beryl's, I'll sort Caitlin out."

Later, as she loaded the dishwasher Evie thought about her mother. Early fifties and single. There had been boyfriends over the years but they had never looked the type to want to join a family. Her mum probably just fancied the wrong type and couldn't or didn't want to change that. She was strong and often said she was not looking for relationships because that wouldn't be fair on herself or him. Evie assumed she had only been in love the once and at the very least felt she should be grateful for that, being the result of that, or the accident of that.

Her half-sister's name was Rebecca. She had drafted a message but had not sent it yet.

"Help me re-arrange the lounge." Jilly said, "Guests will be arriving in half an hour. Martina too."

They moved the dining table against the wall and the second sofa to the patio door then set three rows of five chairs in a line, beginning at the transverse between the doors to the kitchen and the bedrooms, then back to the exterior wall.

"We can stay where we are?" Tom asked.

"Yes of course you can but you are losing the TV now, I'll have to push it back to the wall, give Bob a bit of room." Jilly answered, laughing a little.

"Is he going to stand?" Lou asked, "I've seen him before, I think he sits. Or maybe that was someone else."

Jilly paused mid-fluster to stand beside Evie. "It will do," she said looking at her watch, "don't think I can wait for Daniel. I'll dress Caitlin, then when he gets here he can help me lift her into her chair, won't need the hoist. If you don't tell I won't."

"Sounds fine, Should I get Beryl?"

"Yes, and mention it again to Brian, he won't come so no point wasting too much time with him, but Martina will ask."

Evie looked at the three smiling folk on the sofa. "Good luck with Beryl." Elaine said, "Can't remember the last time I spoke to her."

As she turned a dark blue BMW saloon pulled up outside the front door and she watched as Martina, her assistant Nicky and a tall bald man in a sky-blue rugby shirt she presumed to be the musician got out, they chatted and laughed. Martina was wearing her three-quarter length camel hair coat with blouse and trousers and looked very elegant to Evie. It looked as though things were to start earlier than planned.

"Beryl, we didn't sort out the rest of your newspapers, did we?"

"Eh? That's right dear."

The afternoon outside her window had turned weakly warm and still, the thin nude branches of the sole apple tree glistened in the damp air.

"Are you going to come see Ukulele Bob?"

"Yes dear."

"Shall we get you out of your slippers and into your shoes?"

"Eh? What for?"

"To go into the lounge Beryl"

"No, I like it here."

"To listen to music and maybe sing along."

"That's right dear."

"So, I'll get your shoes."

"Eh?"

Evie tried from another angle. "Lots of folk coming over from the other places, Mirehouse and Hensingham."

"Oh yes dear, can you get me my good cardigan."

"Of course, we need to be quick though to make sure we get you a good seat."

"I know some of those ladies, we go back years you know. I know one of them from school."

As Evie flicked through the rack of clothes in the built-in wardrobe in Beryl's room she listened to the voices coming from the lounge, there were many, the minibus must have dropped off other residents. She nodded and smiled at Daniel as he walked past the doorway of the bedroom. Underneath the voices she could hear a ukulele strum up and down and singing, muffled by the noise at first and then a verse of I'll See You in My Dreams.

Beryl took Evie's arm and slowly they walked down the corridor and into the lounge, Beryl waved at everyone, mouthed greetings and other expressions Evie couldn't quite make sense of as she led her out into the room, she even tried to sashay a little to the music before sitting down on the back row of chairs. She wasn't sure if Beryl recognised any of the visitors or was just trying to show off. "I'll get you a cup of tea in a minute, I've got to go see Brian." As she walked back to the bedrooms the musician began a version of I Saw Her Standing There and several of the audience began to clap along. Evie walked to the end of the corridor to Caitlin's room. "How is it going pet?" asked Jilly, who had just finished brushing the older woman's hair. "You got Beryl into the lounge? Well done you! What do you think?" she added, nodding towards Caitlin who sat smiling in her wheelchair in a pink and cream floral dress and sandals. "Just needs her shawl and we're done."

"I think she looks a very sophisticated lady, did you know it was starting earlier, we've missed two songs already."

"Daniel got a text from Nicky, Ukulele Bob is playing another care home this afternoon so they had to bring it forward half an hour."

"Ok, I'd better have a word with Brian."

"Evie honey, just tell him to be sociable." Jilly put her hand on her shoulder and squeezed, "Stressful day isn't it?"

As she walked back to the closed door to bedroom three, Martina approached. A tall confident woman in her fifties, always well dressed, friendly in what Evie imagined was a professional way for someone whose business was care, good with small talk, and with an extensive memory for personal details.

"I see Caitlin is on her way," she remarked as Daniel pushed her towards them, "Brian?"

"Just going to speak to him now Martina."

"Good, then we need to get refreshments sorted, ok?"

Brian said "Yes?", when she knocked. Used to his taciturnity she took that as permission to go into his room. She found him seated at his small folding desk which he had against the opposite wall from his bed, two neat stacks of books either side of the open one he was staring at. Music played out softly from his CD player, she knew from previous occasions that the woman singing was called Billie Holiday. Seeing how content and engaged he was with his own entertainment she now felt foolish having to ask him whether he wanted to come listen to someone playing popular songs on a ukulele.

He looked over his glasses at her. "You know I won't young lady, but I know you have to ask."

"Don't you ever get lonely, Mr Tate?"

Brian put his book down on the table and took his glasses off. "I try to live as independently as possible, that sometimes comes across as rudeness or me wanting privacy. I don't particularly, I'm just going about my day."

"I know," Evie replied, "just because this room is your home doesn't mean you live in a home. I've heard that's one of your sayings."

"I was an only child you know. Please tell me if I have told you this before, don't want to spend my last years telling the same anecdotes over and over again like that lot out there."

Evie took a step into the room as she didn't want him to think that she didn't have time. "This must be the longest conversation we've ever had, it's normally Jilly you speak to. So, no, you haven't told me this before."

"My parents weren't soft and they didn't have much time for their own families, moved two hundred miles away from where they grew up in Hull. My mother schooled me at home so that was me done for really. Except I learnt how to be happy by myself at a very young age."

"But," said Evie with curiosity, "what about people in your life, partners, children?"

Brian laughed "My wife died many years ago, we never had children. If I'm honest I do regret that. It's what we're all here for isn't it?" Brian picked up his glasses, "Don't misunderstand me though, I really do want to live forever. This is just where we end up when we carry on surviving. I can still read, that's good enough for me."

"I'll just say you were busy then."

Evie closed the door and smiled. She took her mobile phone out of her jeans pocket, half an hour left, no messages. She tapped the icon and called up her draft message to Rebecca and pressed send. The fuss would pass, the fuss was irrelevant. She headed to the kitchen to cut the sponge cake into slivers.

Deadlock

John Field was rushing along Prospect Hill to get back to his flat in time to change and get back out for an interview, simultaneously trying to text as quickly as Jess could text so that he could go back to listening to his music. Yes, he was sorry, no, he shouldn't have snapped at her first thing in the morning. He crossed the road when he reached the estate. The journey back from Finsbury Park had taken longer than he had anticipated, an unplanned delay on the northbound Victoria line, no reason given, just cancellations and delays. He was walking so quickly he no longer felt the sharpness of the breeze through his thin grey suit. So long as it didn't rain he was ok, he could change shirts but not suits. He had taken an afternoon off from his agency assignment doing data entry at Islington Council's Adult Social Care Unit on Upper Street.

What he really wanted was to get himself on a career path with a London council, he was a year from thirty and had always thought of that as a pivotal age. He and Jess had been together for three years and yet they still rented the same one bed flat, couldn't afford a car and struggled to save. He had been temping for a year after not getting on with a couple of attempts at selling since graduating with a degree in Sociology and Politics from Birmingham City University. Meanwhile Jess had ground out six years in packaging design with a family-run dry food importer on the Leeside Estate across the border in Haringey. That was how he had met her, delivering custom-cut cardboard boxes and inserts for Accede. After Birmingham he hadn't wanted to go home to Fleetwood and he had some connection to the capital having two school friends who lived in the city at the time. It seemed to him that only cities offered any prospect of decent employment, his family was not wealthy, they were retired now anyway, and they did not know the type of people who could fix him up with a well-paid job. Islington had introduced him to a part of the public sector where employee benefits meant more than a toilet break, and the salary bands attached to undemanding jobs impressed him. Now he had just over two hours left before he was due at an interview for an Administration Officer position with Parking Services at the London Borough of Waltham Forest. Their main office was on Walthamstow High Street, twenty minutes walk from their flat. The increase in income and the savings on travel could transform their lives. Fifty per cent of their joint income went on rent and council tax, this was an opportunity to change that.

The rain started as he jogged across Shernhall Street and turned heavy just before he went left at Krispy Cottage Chicken and into Turner Road. Water started to soak his right foot. Probably enough time to make a sandwich, have a quick shower, fresh shirt, socks, maybe play a little Battlefield. Three strides up the path to the communal front door, which unlike most other dwellings on the street, had been moved about three feet to the right so that it could open to the stairs to flat 2, and he was home. Closing the door behind him he noticed what looked like a credit card statement addressed to him, balanced on top of the hallway radiator. He glanced up the stairs to flat 2, silence. The McCardell's were out, they worked, they didn't play their music too loud, they had a fleabag cat, he didn't know much more about them. As he was about to slide the key into the lock he noticed that the door was already open. Jess had probably finished early for some reason. "Jess!" He called, walking into the lounge. The flat was compact. Their front door opened directly to a small lounge at the end of which was a door to the kitchen, off the kitchen three further doors, one to the outside yard, one to a small shower room, the other to their bedroom whose ceiling sloped down as the stairs to flat 2 rose above it. There was no answer. The lounge was a bit of a mess. A small wicker basket in which they kept game discs was upended on the two-seat sofa but there were no games in it. He looked at the corner of the room near the window where the TV and the console were kept, and the console was absent. Confused but beginning to feel uneasy he went to the kitchen. His Cambridge CXC CD player and his iPod MP3 were missing from the shelving unit where they kept books, music and other bits and pieces. Everything else was as it should be, no ransacking, not a single door or drawer open. The small yard outside with its sole padlocked brown wooden shed was untouched. John turned and went back to the front door, his heart beating quickly now. Yes, the bolt box on the inside door frame had been forced out an inch, and it was obvious that they had been robbed. What else of value do we have? he thought as he went back to the kitchen, not much. He started opening kitchen cupboards and drawers. Jess had some jewellery. He went to the bedroom. Their pink and blue striped duvet was on the floor by the door and he could smell the toilet, he tried to look at where her trinket box was on the bedside table near the wardrobe but couldn't take his eyes away from the centre of their bed. It didn't make sense, but he was looking at two coiled human turds.

He had to search the police number for non-emergencies on his phone, he wasn't going to report the break-in but what had been left on the bed had bothered him too much. They didn't have a lot worth stealing but to then show contempt for other people's lives in that way made him angry. The officer had said that after talking with a senior colleague they would be opening a case and a beat officer would be in touch soon. He had also been given a crime number he could quote for insurance. They were not insured. He had ninety minutes left before he would have to leave for his interview. Her jewellery was gone, maybe a handbag and some shoes, he wasn't sure about her dresses, nothing of his was missing. The thief had also wiped his backside on a pillow case and thrown it on the floor near their laundry basket. He had tried to call Jess but she hadn't answered so he had sent a message asking her to call when she was available, and telling her about the burglary in the least alarming way he could manage. If she didn't have her MacBook with her then that was gone too.

He checked the shower room if only because it was the one room he hadn't looked in, but nothing had been touched. He looked at himself in the mirror over the beige sink, a bit too much weight these days. He had stopped playing five-a-side football after university. He used to have short hair, now it was over his ears like some really bad tribute to the 1970s. Of necessity their spending habits had changed over the three years. For him clothing and grooming were now unimportant. Only just over eight thousand saved between them but it was a start. They rarely went out now, a weekly takeaway their one luxury. The coming weekend was an exception.

He went back to the kitchen, took off his suit jacket and hung it on the door, sliced a bagel for the toaster and put the kettle on. On Friday night they were going to meet up with his friend Paul and his girlfriend Shima at a sushi bar on Chapel Market and later The Lexington for music and too much beer. It was going to be an expensive night but he had been at Birmingham with Paul. They would always talk about social theory. He had recently finished a book by Mark Fisher and the idea that the twenty-first century had failed to begin, that history ended in the twentieth century, that all of our experiences of the shock of the future were in the past, fascinated him. Social media just made us all too knowing. What had happened to new music? All he heard these days were ironic re-interpretations of someone else. Were you meant to just enjoy music ironically now? He and Paul still got on well, even if he sometimes got the impression that he looked down on him since he had got his PhD and a salary higher than his and Jess's combined. He spread peanut butter over two hot bagel halves and made himself a coffee. Saturday they were travelling across London out to Rickmansworth to visit Jess's parents, overnight stay and back Sunday afternoon. They were probably waiting for him to achieve something too. They owned the laundrette and a dry cleaner's on Barton Way and always talked about their hopes of selling up for a large profit before they retired. They owned a static caravan on the coast near Clacton. It was always a relief when they left Rickmansworth. As he ate he attempted a rough calculation of the value of the things that had been taken from the flat. It was probably less than two thousand pounds. It wouldn't necessarily be a hit on their savings though, he could cope without his CD player and they could always get a second-hand games console quite cheaply, the jewellery he couldn't assess, some of it was from family. He had proposed to Jess over a year ago now, in a bed & breakfast in Moreton-on-the-Marsh in the Cotswolds. She had said she wanted a flat before a wedding.

He checked his phone and the doorbell rang.

The policewoman was young, about his age. "Officer Halfon. Gillian" she said, taking her cap off, "And you are Mr Field, the tenant of Flat 1 who reported the robbery?"

"Yes", he replied, "come in out of the rain."

"I'll need to see some ID Mr Field."

"Of course, won't be a problem," he replied, wondering why he hadn't checked the kitchen drawer with passports and other documents.

"The communal front door was open then, it looks undamaged."

John stared disinterestedly at the door handle, "yeah, I suppose so, must have been left on the catch. I've done it before, neighbours too."

He closed the door, the sky was blackening and the temperature had dropped. There was a course Jess had always wanted to do at Goldsmiths, it usually came up in conversation when they went out but she hadn't talked about it recently when it was just the two of them alone.

"Have you spoken to your neighbours?"

"No answer when I tried before reporting the crime." An MA in Art Psychotherapy, that was it and she should really, he thought, they were both unhappy at work and they shouldn't live out their lives obsessed with income, though at times it felt like that was what they were doing.

"I can knock later," said the policewoman smiling, her radio yapping and hissing away on low volume.

She examined the door to the flat, told him not to touch the basket on the sofa, asked him if he had made a list of items missing, asked if they had encoded their valuables, they had not.

"Why didn't you use your mortice lock, burglar probably would have given up after a few shoulder rams."

"That's my fault, Jess usually does but I was last out this morning. Guess I thought what are the odds of someone getting through two doors."

"Jess is a co-tenant?"

"My girlfriend, yes."

"Well you could try asking your landlord to pay to fix your door but they will probably argue it's down to you because you didn't use the mortice."

"Actually the main thing. The reason I rang you lot was really because of what the thief left behind." He nodded to the officer indicating she should follow and led her to the foot of the bed.

"I see." She said absorbed in her view of the two craps, "It's a bit unusual."

"It's taking the piss, Officer Gillian," said John.

"No. It isn't. Let's go back into the kitchen, we can't just stare at that can we? I've seen similar," she continued, "and I've heard of this but not seen it before."

She declined his offer of coffee so he started to make one for himself.

"An opportunist thief is in a state of nervous excitement and when you've got to go, you've got to go. You don't want to be in a confined space like a toilet where you might not hear the occupier coming back home early, you don't want to be in the lounge and be the first thing the occupier sees so the bedroom sort of makes sense."

"You said you've seen similar?"

"Urine patches."

"Ok."

"Can't make my mind up whether the cast-off duvet was manners or to provide better footing. Probably eliminate manners." She laughed, then apologised.

"So, I guess the main thing is, do we have any chance of getting our stuff back?"

Officer Halfon looked around the kitchen, "There is always a chance. Next thing is for me to talk to my Sergeant and arrange for Scene of Crime to come down here. There have been a few other break-ins in the area. On the other hand your burglar is probably young, stupid and unknown to us or they wouldn't have left a large amount of DNA on your bed. And I'm afraid that means you have to leave things as they are a while longer."

He put his coffee down as he realised she was finished and about to leave.

"How long before the next person arrives, do you think?"

"Could be a few hours, but before 6pm." Outside the door to his flat she stopped and looked up the stairs. "I'll just give your neighbours a try."

John looked at his watch. It was too late to reschedule the interview.

"What are their names?" Officer Halfon asked as she rapped twice on their door.

"McCardell."

"Can't hear any noise and the door is undamaged," she noted. "Ok, I'll need you to come down to Forest Road to add to your statement, this evening or tomorrow, just quote your crime number at the desk. Provide us with an email address and you'll be able to track your crime online. Ok Mr Field, nice to have met you."

And she was gone. He looked back into his flat, the faded green carpet, the second hand blue and white striped two seat sofa they got from Murphy's Second Chance Warehouse, the beige wallpapered walls, the beige ceiling. Jess had grown up in the two flats above her parents' shops and that was why she was so determined to get a mortgage on her own place. There was no way past it, they would just have to put things on hold for a couple of years. He went back in. He found a can of air freshener in the shower room, sprayed the bedroom and closed the door. Changed his mind, went back into the bedroom, loosened the bed sheet at the corners and drew it and its contents into a bundle before carrying it through to the kitchen and dropping it into a refuse sack. He took a bottle of bleach from beneath the kitchen sink, poured a little onto the dishcloth, then went back to the mattress and rubbed the damp patch. He threw the cloth on the floor next to the pillowcase and wrestled the mattress over to its other, less soiled side. He scooped up the pillow case and the cloth and put them in the sack with the sheet. He took a fresh sheet from the chest of drawers, fitted it quickly and flung the duvet back on the bed.

He looked at his watch, there was no time left. He took a black umbrella from the wardrobe, got his suit jacket and his phone, used the mortice lock on the door and stepped out into the cold darkness of Turner Road. The rain had stopped and in the stillness the smell of pavement, tarmac and petrol oozed upwards. He got to Shernhall Street and crossed to Church Hill Road before his phone rang and his favourite photograph of Jess backlit itself and she was smiling at him, her mischievous brown eyes, her half smile. He told her what had happened.

"No, it wasn't a death threat." He laughed. He walked past the grim estates at the top of Church Hill Road. "Because I've got to get to the interview." She had a habit of getting to the point. "But I've bagged it, they can have the bag." Sometimes even when she laughed she was deadly serious. "You forget to use both locks now and again." When she was upset her feelings made her stick on things. "Sorry, I thought you did, I didn't know that. I genuinely thought you had forgotten before." He knew not to push her on to something else. "I didn't think it was likely, it is my fault, I'm sorry." Gently it started to rain, fine like lines of morse code through the orange orbs of the street lights. "It was your grandmother's, I know. You were very close…yes." You fall in love and then you pay into it he thought, you pay an extortionate price for even the basic model of being with someone. You pay in non-cash ways, too. In time apart, in being frustrated in the efforts you make to give yourselves a good life. Little by little you abandon all the things that make you individual, all the things you wanted to do, as though it were ballast and you might make it higher without them. "I know baby. I'll get this job. Next year or two a promotion…you can do that course. It's just a bit of bad luck baby. I love you Jess." He shook open his umbrella. "I don't want you to do that either. I'll meet you at the station after…ok…you text me then and tell me where you are."

He turned right onto Church Hill and after a few further minutes walking he could see the white light of the High Street in the distance, it shimmered as traffic flowed past well-lit buildings, the disjointed tube of light vibrated as if were substantial.

Printed in Great Britain
by Amazon